The Tiger's Stripes

Written by Graham Marks • Illustrated by Stephen Holmes

SHOOTING STAR PRESS

The Tiger's Stripes

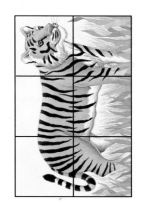

Long, long ago in the forests of India, lived a huge orange cat. He was very big and had beautiful sharp teeth and claws and a long tail. He was very proud indeed of his gleaming fur and was always boasting to all the other animals in the forest.

"I must be the most beautiful creature in the whole world," the cat would say to them. "No other creature has such a fine orange coat as me."

The cat strutted around the forest until he met a peacock, its wonderful fan of blue-green feathers covered in shining eyes.

"Good morning cat," said the peacock, "don't you think my feathers are looking splendid today?"

"Oh! They are splendid feathers, but not nearly so fine as my shining orange coat," replied the cat proudly.

The sun was beginning to get hot and the cat was getting thirsty, so he went down to the river for a drink. When he reached the river and stooped to drink, he saw his own reflection in the clear water.

"I say! What a handsome fellow I am!" exclaimed the cat boastfully. Just then a huge green crocodile appeared nearby, the sunlight gleaming on its scaly back, so it shone like jewels.

"Beautiful day, cat," said the crocodile. "Just look how the sun shines on my beautiful scales."

"Your scales are indeed very fine, crocodile," replied the cat, "but not nearly so fine as my bright orange fur."

The crocodile was tired of listening to the cat boasting and so he sank slowly out of sight back into the water, leaving the boastful cat all alone.

After the cat had eaten, he went to sleep for a long time. The bright sun was burning down and the long waving grass cast dark

shadows on his orange coat. The sun was so hot that as he slept it began to burn his orange fur.

Later the cat awoke from his sleep and went down to the river to drink. As he looked down into the water he saw a very strange sight. His bright orange coat was now striped with black, where it had been burnt by the hot sun.

And from that day on, the tiger, as he is now known, has a coat of orange and black stripes, from his nose to the very tip of his long tail.

Now that you have enjoyed the story of how the tiger got his stripes, you can make your own tiger jigsaw block picture of the boastful tiger in his striped coat of orange and black. Put your jigsaw block picture of the tiger together and you'll soon be in the hot forest of India. But, do take care and beware of boastful tigers!

The Duck Who Wouldn't Grow Up

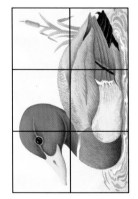

It was Spring and Mrs Mallard was very happy that all eleven eggs in her nest looked like they were just about to hatch.

In fact they did just that the very next day. One by one little beaks tapped at the shells and cracked them open.

Out into the world, one by one, came eleven tiny balls of fluff. Mrs Mallard was delighted! Her ducklings looked perfect, every single one of them.

But as the days passed she noticed that, while ten of her babies were doing all the things they should, the eleventh wasn't.

"Number Eleven," Mrs Mallard would say (she gave them all numbers because she couldn't possibly think of eleven different names), "come along now, Number Eleven, eat up your weeds or you'll never grow up big and strong like your father!"

But Number Eleven didn't really want to grow up to be big and strong. If he did, he'd have to start swimming in the river! He couldn't do that, he would probably sink!

And worse still, if he grew up, he'd have to start flying! Just thinking about it made him shiver with fear. No, thought little Number Eleven, he wasn't going to be doing anything quite so silly as growing up.

As the ducklings grew bigger and bigger, One, Two, Three, Four, Five, Six, Seven, Eight, Nine and Ten all began going off with their father for swimming lessons, leaving Number Eleven by himself in the nest.

"Don't worry about me," he called after them. "I'll be all right—I'll have it all nice and tidy for when you come back!"

As he was throwing some rubbish from the nest into the river he saw something huge flash silver in the water—something huge with lots and lots of sharp teeth!

He'd heard his father warn them about nasty fish that liked to eat ducklings, and there it was now, going off after his family!

"Quack! Quack!! QUACK!!!" went Number Eleven, but his family were too far away to hear him. "What can I do?" he sobbed, running down the river bank, flapping his wings as he went.

Flap, flap, flap went his wings, harder and harder the faster he ran. Then the most extraordinary thing happened—he found his feet were off the ground and he was flying! Really flying!

For a moment he was terrified, and nearly fell, but then he saw his family, with the huge silver fish not far behind them! He swooped down towards them.

"Danger!" he yelled. "Get onto the river bank! A big fish is coming!"

Instantly Mr Mallard hurried his ten ducklings out of the water. Number Eleven flew down and landed on the riverbank.

"You can fly!" beamed his father.

"I was in such a hurry to warn you, I must have forgotten to be frightened," said little Number Eleven.

Now you've read the story, use your jigsaw blocks to make the picture of the duck. Is it a picture of Number Eleven's father, or is it him when he's grown up? Now he's not frightened any more, he can eat his weeds and grow up big and strong, just like his father.

The Frog's Princess

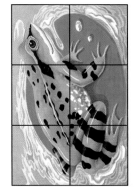

It was a bright sunny day down by the pond and the frog was feeling very happy. He had just found the pond, with clouds of tasty insects to eat and lots of comfy lily pads to sit on and croak. Everything, he thought, was just about perfect.

"Ribbett!" said the frog, "this is a wonderful place, even if there aren't any other frogs to talk to."

Just then he spotted a young girl coming to play in the gardens. She was very pretty, all dressed in a fine, white dress, with beautiful flowers woven into her long golden hair.

"My goodness!" thought the frog, "I wonder who she could be?"

He watched her playing in the garden and thought she was the most beautiful thing he'd ever seen.

The frog was very sad when the girl left the garden, but to his great delight, she came back the very next day. In fact, every day when the sun was shining, the beautiful girl would come to play by the pond in the garden.

And every day the frog would sit on a lily pad and gaze at her. Although he loved to watch the girl playing, as the days passed, he became more lonely.

"What's the matter?" asked a fish, who lived in the pond. "You look very sad."

"I am," replied the frog, "I'm the only frog in this pond and I'm lonely. I can only sit here on my lily pad and watch the girl playing in the garden. She's pretty enough to be a princess."

"If she is a princess, perhaps she could kiss you and turn you into a prince," said the big fish.

"But I'm just a frog!" said the frog, "I'm not a prince!"

"How do you know?" the fish said, "if a wicked witch had cast a spell on you, you WOULD think you were just a frog, wouldn't you?"

"Who knows, you could be right," said the frog. "I wouldn't remember, would I?"

"Of course not!" smiled the fish.

"But what should I do?" groaned the frog, "how can I get her to kiss me?"

"Well you won't do anything sitting here on your lily pad, will you?" said the fish.

So the frog leaped out of the water and hopped to where the girl was sitting.

He puffed out his chest and croaked as loudly as he could, "Ribbett! Ribbett!"

The girl looked down and saw him. "Oh what a handsome frog!" she said, gently picking him up. "I wonder, are you really a handsome prince that some wicked witch cast a spell on?" she added with a laugh and bending down, she gently kissed him.

There was puff of colored smoke and suddenly the girl was gone and two frogs were sitting side by side on the grass.

"Oh! I've turned into a frog," said the girl.

"So you have, and a very pretty frog indeed," replied the other frog.

"Ha ha! You may not be a prince," laughed the big fish, popping his head up out of the water, "but at least you won't be lonely any more."

What a surprise for the frog, and for the little girl. Now you've read this story you can make your own frog jigsaw block picture of the handsome frog, or is it really the little girl? Remember in future, although you must always be kind to all creatures, especially frogs, perhaps it's not a very good idea to kiss them!

Young Owl Tries to Help!

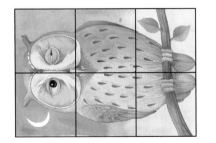

Of all the animals that lived in the forest by far the most big-headed was Young Owl. He always thought he knew everything and would say what he thought, even if he wasn't asked.

When Squirrel couldn't find the nuts he'd hidden in the Autumn, it was Young Owl who said, "If you'd tied a knot in your hankie I'm sure you wouldn't have forgotten, Squirrel old thing!"

When Mole got lost in one of his own tunnels it was Young Owl who said, "I know what you need. You need to get yourself a pair of glasses, Moley old chap!"

When Woodpecker had a bad headache one day it was Young Owl who said, "You really should be using a hammer and chisel instead of your beak—you'll feel a lot better if you have a little lie down!"

Everyone had become really rather tired of Young Owl and his clever ideas. It was getting so you couldn't do anything without Young Owl telling you how to do it better.

The trouble was, he was Old Owl's son, and Old Owl was the wisest animal in the forest. He was the creature you always went to with your problems. He was the one who almost always knew the answers.

So, who was going to tell Old Owl that

his son was big-headed and should keep his clever ideas to himself? There was no one in the forest who dared.

One day Young Owl was out in the forest when he came across a little Wren crying. "What's the matter?" he asked. He was sure he could solve any problem the tiny bird might have.

"Where's your father?" she said crossly.

"I'm here," said a deep voice from inside the tree. "What can I do to help?"

"You can stop your son from telling everyone what to do!" said Robin. "That's what you can do! Did you know he told the Wren to build her nest on the ground, and now her eggs have been stolen!"

Without waiting for an answer Robin flew away. Old Owl sighed, shook his head and looked sadly at his son.

"What did I do wrong, Father?" said the puzzled Young Owl. "I was only trying to help, like you do."

"It's always good to try and help, but sometimes the wisest thing of all is to admit that you really don't know the answer," said wise Old Owl.

"I'm having trouble building my nest," the little Wren sobbed. "Every time I think I've finished, it falls out of the tree—I shall never be able to lay my eggs!"

"What you should do is build it on the ground," said Young Owl, "then it can't fall anywhere, can it?"

"Do you think it will be all right?" asked the Wren.

"Of course," said Young Owl, flapping his wings and flying away, "no problem!"

Some time later Young Owl was perched by his home when Robin flew up, looking very angry indeed.

Young Owl was only trying to help, but it all went wrong. I wonder if he has learned his lesson now and has stopped trying to tell the other animals what to do. Now you've read the story, get your jigsaw blocks out and see if you can make the picture of Old Owl. Do you think he looks very wise? If you have trouble making the picture, I'm sure someone will try to help you, just like Young Owl.

The Unlucky Cat

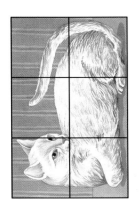

The cat lay curled up on the mat, outside the door of the house. She was a beautiful white cat, white as the new fallen snow, white as summer clouds.

She thought she was the luckiest cat alive to be so white, so perfect.

"I'm so glad I'm not a boring stripy tabby or a horrid ginger color," she thought to herself, as the sun shone on her fur.

She began cleaning herself, even though she didn't need to. As she licked one of her delicate paws, a chirpy little bird flew down and perched nearby.

"You must have to spend hours cleaning yourself," chirped the bird. "Don't you ever get bored?"

"No," replied the white cat, "as I'm lucky enough to be a beautiful white cat I should keep myself as clean as possible."

"Oh," said the bird, "I thought black cats were supposed to be the lucky ones."

The white cat stopped licking her paw and looked at the bird. "That," she replied, "is just a silly fairy tale."

"I don't believe you," said the bird.

"Believe what you like," the cat replied, as she stood up and arched her back. "I've got better things to do than waste my time talking to you."

"Well I don't think white cats are lucky," said the bird, flying off, "I think they're just big-headed!"

"Cheek!" muttered the cat, watching the bird fly away out of reach. She didn't chase after birds, just in case she got her coat dirty.

With nothing else to do, the cat decided to go up onto the roof. From there she could see everything that was going on in the neighborhood.

Going round to the side of the house she jumped onto the rain barrel, up on the little canopy over the side door and then up onto the roof itself.

Walking carefully up the tiles she ended her journey perched right on top of the wide chimney pot.

The view was wonderful—she could see for miles—and the cat sat looking down on the world below her. She paid no attention at all to the sky above her.

She didn't hear anything until it was far too late. The seagull, up in town on a day trip from the seashore, swooped down out of the bright blue sky and playfully swiped the cat with his wing.

He'd only meant to scare the cat, but he knocked her straight into the open chimney. It all happened so quickly that the cat didn't have a chance to do a thing. One moment she was enjoying the view, the next she was

falling down a long, dark tunnel.

She landed with a thud in the fireplace, far below, with soot flying everywhere.

"Atishoo!" sneezed the cat. "Oh, I'm covered in soot! I'd better go outside and get cleaned up."

As she walked out into the garden she saw her reflection in the glass door—she was completely black with soot, from the tip of her nose to her paws!

"There you are! I told you that white cats weren't lucky," laughed the bird, from his perch nearby.

This story just goes to show that it doesn't pay to be too proud of yourself. I'm sure that the white cat didn't feel very lucky when she fell down the chimney and got covered in soot. Now get your jigsaw blocks and try to make the picture of the cat. But remember, if you do it, don't be too proud of yourself!

Giraffe's Neck

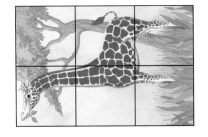

One day, long ago a strange-looking creature called a giraffe wandered into a place he'd never been to before. He was strange-looking because he had very long legs and an extremely short neck.

He was not a clever creature, but he was very, very curious. One day he came to a wall of tall bushes and could go no further.

No matter how hard he tried he could not see through the thick wall of leaves and he was not tall enough to see over the top.

Being a very, very curious creature, this began to make him angry. More than anything else in the whole world the giraffe wanted to see what was on the other side of the bushes.

He watched the birds flying over the bushes with the greatest of ease, but he had no wings, so he couldn't do that.

He saw gazelles and leopards jump over the bushes, but he was no good at jumping, so he couldn't do that.

He saw monkeys climb up and swing, chattering through the branches, but he didn't have fingers or toes to grip, so he couldn't do that.

The more he watched the creatures either

flying, jumping or climbing over the tall bushes, the more curious he became to see what it was on the other side.

"I wish I could see what's on the other side of these bushes," the giraffe said to himself, craning his short neck.